...VABLE OLIVER AND THE SAWED-IN-HALF DADS

WRITTEN BY

PSEUDONYMOUS BOSCH

ILLUSTRATED BY

Shane Pangburn

DIAL BOOKS FOR YOUNG READERS

For the Phenomenal Phillip —P.B.
For my Marvelous Mom and Dependable Dad —S.P.

Dial Books for Young Readers
An imprint of Penguin Random House LLC, New York

Text copyright © 2020 by Pseudonymous Bosch
Illustrations copyright © 2020 by Shane Pangburn

Visit us online at penguinrandomhouse.com

Library of Congress Cataloging-in-Publication Data is available.

Printed in the United States of America
ISBN 9780525552352

1 3 5 7 9 10 8 6 4 2

Design by Jennifer Kelly
Text set in Adobe Text Pro

The Program

INTRODUCTION (The Invitation) 1

Chapter One: The Grand Cake Tasting 7

Chapter Two: Bon Voyage 20

Chapter Three: Magic Shopping 28

Chapter Four: The Rehearsal for the Rehearsal Brunch . . . 40

Chapter Five: Showtime! 49

Chapter Six: What Did We Forget? 62

Chapter Seven: Define *Missing* 68

Chapter Eight: Runaways 80

Chapter Nine: Hostage Negotiations 89

Chapter Ten: Rabbit Run 100

Chapter Eleven: From Maze to Mansion 107

Chapter Twelve: Secret Passages 115

Chapter Thirteen: Guests and Guesses 126

Chapter Fourteen: Getting Ready (to Call It Off) 137

Chapter Fifteen: Rabbit Down the Hole 145

Chapter Sixteen: Cutting the Cake 151

Chapter Seventeen: The Reception 167

AFTER-PARTY (How to Perform Oliver's Trick) 193

INTRODUCTION

Welcome.
How wonderful to see you.

You're here for a book. Am I right?

Don't ask how I knew.
An author never reveals his secrets.

Do you want to read it now?

Very well. The book is yours.
Just say the magic words.

No, not *please* or *thank you*.
Not even *abracadabra*.
Just say . . . *I do*.

Did you say it? Good.
You may now kiss the book.

Oh, did I say *kiss* the book?
I meant *read* the book.
You're not marrying it!

R.S.V.P.

Kindly Respond by April 1st

Name(s): **Bea & Teenie**
~~TEENIE & BEA~~

Plus one : OLIVER

☑ **It was our idea!** Accepts with pleasure
☐ Declines with regrets

Please check all that apply:
☐ Meat-free ☐ Dairy-free ☐ Gluten-free
☐ Nut-free ☐ ~~Sugar-free~~ → Never!
☐ There's no such thing as a free lunch.

The Grand Cake Tasting

"Try this one."

The twins, Bea and Teenie, had insisted that Oliver come with them to the cake tasting.

"He's a cake expert," Bea told their fathers. "He'll be a big help."

"Yeah, he really, really loves cake," said Teenie.

So far, Oliver hadn't been even a tiny help. He loved each cake equally. Each flavor got the highest possible score.

The twins' fathers were beside themselves. Of all the wedding planning they'd had to do, the cake tasting was supposed to be the easy part. "Why, oh why did we bring the children into this?" Simon asked (just as he'd asked when they debated the dinner menu and the flowers and the music).

Miguel tried to make the best of the situation.

"Now, Oliver," he said. "Isn't there one cake that you prefer?"

"Nope," Oliver said with his mouth full. "They're all perfect. Thanks for taking me here, Mr. Dad and Mr. Papa."

Oliver never knew what names to call adults. He just went with what Bea and Teenie called them. Plus *Mr.* to be polite.

"Simon and Miguel is fine," Simon told Oliver, not for the first time.

"Okay, Mr. Simon and Mr. Miguel."

"No, I meant just—oh, never mind."

The girls weren't helping much either. Having given up on choosing the cake's flavor, they had decided to focus on design. They were leafing through a binder full of more and more extravagant cakes.

Cakezilla

Just Frosting

Under the Sea Salt and Caramel

Leaning Cake of Pieces

Teenie held up a photo of a pirate ship. It had licorice cannons, a candy-cane mast, a marzipan sail, and a giant gummy squid attacking the deck.

"That one floats," the baker chimed in.

Jacques Fondant had been a baker to the stars for twenty years now. He'd designed cakes for YouTubers, presidents, and reality-show hosts. But he never let it go to his head. He still made cakes for anyone and everyone. No cake too small or too big.

The twins wanted a big cake.

"Can this one have more floors?" Bea had started sketching their dream dessert, which looked something like a Japanese pagoda crossed with the Empire State Building. She taped two sheets together for height.

"You mean more *stories*?" asked Teenie as Bea climbed onto Teenie's shoulders to properly display her creation.

"The word is *tiers*, but forget about that," said Miguel. "We want something simple."

"Vanilla buttercream," Simon added. "Two tiers."

"UGH! THEN WHAT'S THE POINT?" Bea theatrically fell from her sister's shoulders.

"Girls," Miguel said, "we're glad you want to help, but this is *our* wedding."

"WAIT!" Oliver nearly spat out one of three bites of cake he was currently chewing.

YOU TWO AREN'T ALREADY MARRIED?

Oliver had known Simon and Miguel his whole life. Of course they were married. They had children. They shared a house and a car.

"I know," said Bea. "Can you believe it? In the olden days, two dads couldn't get married."

"It's kind of like how they didn't use to have cell phones," Teenie explained. "Now they can marry and we're finally making it official."

"*We* are," Miguel specified. "The fathers."

"And we'd like you to be the ring bearer!" said Teenie.

Oliver had never been to a wedding and his only knowledge of ring bearers came from *The Lord of the Rings*. It seemed like too much responsibility. "I couldn't, honestly. I can't bear anything."

"Nonsense," said Simon. "You'll do great. And the girls will be there to help."

"That's right!" said Bea. "We're going to be flower girls. Or flower scientists, really."

"Well, she's a flower scientist," said Teenie. "I'm a flower assassin."

Oliver was confused. "So you kill flowers?"

"Right. I pick them off one by one. And we're both ..."

The girls attempted a drumroll on their empty plates. (It ended up being more of a *crumb* roll.)

"Magician's assistants," announced Teenie.

"Magician's *executive* assistants," amended Bea.

"But there's no magician. W-wait . . ." Oliver stammered, realizing the terrifying implications of this. "You want me . . . at your dads' . . . ?"

They nodded, smiling.

Bea and Teenie considered themselves managers of local magic talent the Unbelievable Oliver. Their friend was in high demand after the rousing success at their classmate Maddox's ninth birthday party three months before.

"We're getting dozens of requests, Oliver," said Bea. "DOZENS!"

"But we thought it was only fair to give our dads your first—well, second—official show!" said Teenie.

Their dads looked at each other.

"It's not that we don't want our wedding to be magical," said Miguel gently. "We do. It's just—"

"It's just that it's *our* wedding," Simon finished.

"But it was *our* idea!" protested Bea. "You were going to go to City Hall."

"Well, it's *our* idea now," Miguel said. "You gave it to us."

"Exactly," Simon agreed. "So no magic tricks. And a simple two-tier—"

Oliver wanted to be polite, but he too wanted a larger cake, so he just grumbled "more cake please" under his breath. The baker, who was similarly at a loss for words, slipped him a piece.

"Fine, three tiers," Simon said, to stop the girls' shouting. "Vanilla Velvet—"

"Double Chocolate!"

"Strawberry Bubblegum!"

"Four tiers," Simon compromised. "Cherry Jubilee, Caramel Sunset, After-Dark Chocolate, and Passionate Passion Fruit. But no more."

The girls made their saddest puppy dog faces, which they had perfected by practicing in the mirror. Teenie could even cry on command.

But the two dads had practiced as well, challenging each other to resist all sad faces. Miguel, a photographer, had even made flash cards. Simon, who wrote the words for advertisements, had added dialogue:

The brave fathers were immune to further demands and the girls knew four tiers was the most they were going to get.

"Deal," Bea said, holding out her hand.

To make it official, Teenie spat on her hand before extending it. "AND a magic show."

"NO! Not at the wedding," said Miguel.

"But we worked out a whole routine," said Bea. "It's incredible. You should see: the Unbelievable Oliver, the Brilliant Beatriz, and the Marvelous Martina."

This was news to Oliver.

"We're still working on the names," Teenie said. She didn't like being called Martina, even a marvelous one.

"No, absolutely not," said Simon.

"Please . . . please . . . please . . . please . . . please . . . We're going to keep saying it . . . please . . . please . . ."

"Well, maybe at the rehearsal brunch," Miguel said.

Bea raised a fist in victory. "Yes!"

"And at least five tiers!" added Teenie, fist-bumping her sister.

"Do you have an extra piece of carrot cake for my friend?" Oliver asked the baker as the others made their way out.

If he was going to do another magic show, he was going to need help.

Help from somebody who loved carrots almost as much as Oliver loved cake.

Bon Voyage

From the bed, Oliver could reach his desk or really any part of his room, including the ceiling if he jumped. His bedroom was small, but it filled all of Oliver's needs: a rack for his jacket and top hat, a drawer for his three identical shirts and seven pairs of underwear (one for each day of the week), and another drawer for his slowly growing collection of magic supplies.

Today, his desk was crowded with printouts of various magic tricks, all well beyond his skill level.

A rabbit lounged on the bed nearby, surrounded by carrot cake crumbs. Contented, he made a sound that might have been a burp or a fart. (With a rabbit, it's sometimes hard to tell.)

"Can't we just do a card trick?" Oliver asked. "The Four Jokers was a big hit last time."

"A modest hit," the rabbit, who was named Benny, corrected him. "You've got to go bigger this time!"

He tossed off a few ideas, each more alarming than the last.

"Oliver, you don't actually saw anybody in half. That's why they call it a *trick*."

"What if I just pull you out of a hat?"

"I'm a professional, Ollie. Not just something you pull out of a hat. I'm not dandruff!"

In fact, when Oliver met Benny, the rabbit had been living in a hat. (The longtime magician's rabbit had just escaped from Las Vegas and was hiding out in the hat when Oliver bought it at a local magic shop.) But Oliver didn't think it would be nice to correct him.

"Besides, I won't be there," said Benny. "One wedding was enough for me! And a magician never gets top billing. It's all about the sappy couple getting married."

"I thought it was *happy* couple. What does *sappy* mean?"

With the barest hint of a knock, Oliver's mother opened his bedroom door. Oliver shook his head, trying to cut Benny off, but once the rabbit started on weddings, he really got on a roll.

"You know, sappy. Syrupy. Corny."

Oliver's mother, Diane, held a load of laundry, fresh and warm from the dryer. She tossed it on the bed and, mercifully, over Benny.

"Help me fold these clothes, please," she said. "Who were you talking to just now?"

"No bunny, Mom." Oliver slapped his forehead. "I mean, *no-body*."

As Oliver's mother sorted laundry, a single T-shirt mysteriously crept off the edge of the bed.

"I must be hearing things," she said. "I need a vacation. You want to go on a cruise, Oliver?"

23

"Sure."

"Aw, who needs a cruise? I'm just glad I have a weekend off for once. Thank goodness for this wedding. Told the hospital I'm out of town. Can't be reached. A whole weekend off, Oliver. Can you imagine?"

Oliver folded a shirt in one swift motion. "I *can* imagine."

Before Bea and Teenie had started booking him as a magic act, Oliver had had nearly every weekend off. At his mother's insistence, he'd tried T-ball, basketball, and even ballroom dancing. But, thankfully, he failed at most extracurricular activities.

Besides, his mother was almost always too busy to drop him off. Except for Hebrew school. (For some reason, she was never too busy to take him to Hebrew school.) So he had plenty of weekends to himself, practicing home-based hobbies, like magic and folding laundry.

He'd gotten very good at it. Laundry, that is. Not magic.

OLIVER'S LAUNDRY TIPS

1 Pinch shirt at shoulder and chest.

2 Move right hand to hem. Pinch fabric below also. Do not move left hand.

3 Uncross your arms and lift the shirt like so . . .

4 Then lay it down to fold one more time, and VOILA!

OH?! YOU CAN DO THAT, BUT YOU CAN'T DO A SIMPLE ROPE TRICK OR EVEN TIE YOUR SHOES!

"Well, I'm off to visit the living room. I may even sit down. A whole weekend, Oliver!"

Oliver waved goodbye to his mother and wiped his sweating brow with an unfolded sock.

"Benny, that was close. Do you think she suspects that you can talk?"

"I suspect she does, kid. That woman is a lot smarter than you."

"Well, what do we do?" Oliver asked.

The rabbit nodded thoughtfully. "Good question. If she finds out about me, she might make me pay rent. And between you and me, my credit isn't too good. We better play it cool."

With another nearly silent knock, Oliver's mother entered the room again, and handed him another load of laundry.

HOP

HOP

@$%!

"Oliver," she said. "What's going on? I could swear I heard that rabbit swear."

"Oh, Benny never swears." Oliver slapped his forehead again. "Or talks. How could he swear? He can't talk. He's a rabbit."

"I must be going mad," said his mother. "Maybe it runs in the family. You're talking to yourself. I'm hearing things."

Diane picked up the rabbit off the floor and deposited him on the bed.

"Well, you and your rabbit are on your own preparing for this show. My vacation starts now. Bon voyage."

Oliver scratched his head. "Isn't that what I'm supposed to say to you?"

Magic Shopping

Oliver didn't want to go to the Great Zoochee-ni's Magic Emporium. Not after what the Great Zoocheeni did to them at Maddox's party, framing Oliver and the twins for Grand Theft Robot. It was only through clever casework and magic that they'd cleared their names, confronted the guilty parties, and found the stolen birthday present.*

"You're still mad about that?" Teenie said. "It was months ago. Almost."

_____

* You can read all about it in *The Unbelievable Oliver and the Four Jokers*, available wherever books are sold. If you're looking for a birthday gift nobody will steal, might I suggest a book? Maybe two?

"And besides," Bea added, "it's the only magic shop in town."

"And Papa says we should support local businesses."

Oliver couldn't argue with the twins, their papa, AND the value of local entrepreneurship.

In the short time since his last visit, the Great Zoocheeni's Magic Emporium had somehow grown shabbier. It seemed like there was an extra year's worth of dust on the rubber chickens and Magic 8-Balls.

Once the door chimes woke him up, Oliver's cousin Spencer greeted them with a yawn. "'Sup, Oliver, Beatriz, Martina. Let me know if you need any help."

"Look—don't our dads need those?" Bea nodded toward a row of dusty neckties hanging next to a few old Halloween costumes.

"Definitely! They love Halloween," said Teenie, picking out one tie with a spider pattern and another decorated with worms. "These will be perfect for the wedding."

"Oh, hey, what about the music?" asked Spencer.

He was going to be the DJ for the wedding, as well as the valet parker and  Miguel's photo assistant. At any given time, Spencer worked about seventeen jobs. He was trying to buy a car and also to create an app that would connect young video game players with corporate sponsors.

"Are your dads more into house or trap?"

The twins blinked.

"Norwegian death metal?"

"They really like embarrassing us," noted Bea. "What music do you have that's embarrassing?"

"Plenty. Take a look."

Spencer showed his playlist to the girls, who began choosing tracks that played just loud enough to disguise a conversation between Oliver and his rabbit.

"Okay, Benny," said Oliver over his shoulder. "What do we need to get? Oh, rings."

He picked up a pair of large linked magician's rings.

Benny had hidden in Oliver's hat the whole way to the store. He too wanted nothing to do with Zoocheeni, but he knew Oliver would be helpless without him. He lifted the hat just enough to whisper in Oliver's ear.

"Rings at a wedding? How original! Next you'll want flowers."

"Flowers? That's the girls' job," said Oliver, not picking up on the rabbit's sarcasm.

"Ask about the sawed-in-half trick," suggested Benny. "I promise there won't be any blood."

"Not even fake blood?"

"What's that, Oliver?" Spencer asked.

"Um . . ." Oliver was still nervous about using sharp tools onstage, but he didn't want Spencer to think he was talking to himself. "Do you have the sawed-in-half trick?"

"Yes!" exclaimed Spencer with something close to excitement. "I almost never have what a customer asks for, but . . ."

With an almost dramatic flourish, he pulled an old, moth-eaten blanket off a long, black coffin-shaped box.

"It's a pretty simple trick," Spencer said. "Do I have any volunteers to slip into this coffin?"

Teenie and Bea raised their hands.

"Do we get to die first?" asked Teenie hopefully.

"Only after you're inside. Okay, as you can see, this coffin is actually two boxes put together." Spencer opened the lid of one of the boxes. "First, Martina, you get inside this box here and hide. That's before the curtain rises. Nobody knows about you, okay? Can you guys keep a secret?"

"I don't know," said Teenie as she climbed into the box. "I thought my real name was a secret, but I guess it isn't." She glared meaningfully at Bea.

"Bea, you're onstage in front of the audience," said Spencer. "You get in the other box, leaving your head sticking out of this hole here. You have to bend your legs to fit."

Bea did her best to squeeze into the other box.

Spencer turned back to Teenie.

"Martina, stick your legs out of the other end . . . See, now everyone will think it's one coffin with one girl inside, but it's actually Bea's head and Martina's feet.

"Then when Oliver saws the coffin in half, like so . . ." Spencer handed Oliver an oversized plastic saw. "Go on, Oliver."

Oliver poked hesitantly at the coffin. The saw wobbled noisily.

"Really put your back into it," Benny whispered. "You're sawing your friend in half—it shouldn't just tickle."

Oliver still wasn't getting it. So Spencer grabbed his hand and forced Oliver to slice through the two boxes in a single stroke.

"AAAAAAAH!" Bea screamed. "My legs. You sawed off my precious legs."

"I'm sorry!"
Oliver was terrified.
"I thought it was
just a trick! Spencer, call 911!"

Teenie swung her box open, and everyone in the room stared at Oliver. Even Benny lifted the brim of the hat and looked down at him with incredulity.

"Oh, I guess the trick works." Oliver laughed weakly. "We'll take it."

"Great," Spencer said. "Um, how are you gonna pay?"

Bea stuck her hand out of the hole at the side of the box. She held a $100 bill.

"We have a one-hundred-dollar magic budget from our dads."

At the reveal of such a large bill, the back door opened and the owner of the shop, the Great Zoocheeni him-self, practically flew into the room. His dove, Paloma, flew in beside him.

"A wedding, you say? *All*-liver, you're doing weddings now?" Zoocheeni pretended he didn't know how to pronounce Oliver's name. "Of course, there's only so much money in birthday parties. Now, a wedding. You could make a fortune. Two or even three hundred dollars."

"Yeah," said Oliver, although *any* money was a fortune to him.

"Well, that trick is purrrfect for a wedding," purred Zoocheeni. "Sawing a beloved partner in half is considered very good luck. But I'm sorry, it's not for sale. I have a sentimental attachment to . . . detaching people's limbs."

Bea's head and Teenie's legs drooped in disappointment.

"Now, we do have another one available to rent." Zoocheeni pointed to a second, more dilapidated coffin, with bits of duct tape around the edges. This coffin, like the other, was on wheels, and it squeaked as he turned it toward the children.

"This coffin alone, for a whole weekend in peak

wedding season—well, that would be five hundred dollars."

"But our dads only gave us one hundred," said Bea. "And we want to get two ties."

Zoocheeni nodded and the dove snatched the hundred out of Bea's hand. Paloma flew the bill up to one of the few overhead lights in the dim store. She nodded as if to say "It's real all right."

"Well, perhaps we could do the coffin and ties for ninety-five dollars," Zoocheeni said. "But the dolly will cost extra."

"They need the dolly," Spencer pointed out. "It's part of the trick."

He was right. In order for the illusion to work, the boxes sat on a specially designed cart that concealed part of each performer.

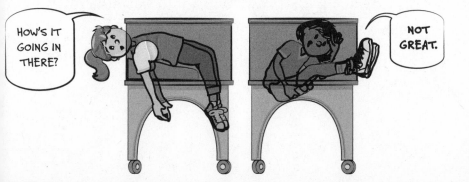

"Fine, one hundred all in," Zoocheeni agreed without enthusiasm. "Now, where does this need to be delivered to?"

"Hauntington Gardens," Bea said.

"Ah, yes, the old Hauntington estate," said Zoocheeni. "A nice venue for a séance—once upon a time. Seen better days, I'm afraid. Still, for a funeral—"

"Wedding!" Teenie interjected.

"And it's *still* nice," said Bea.

She was excited to visit the gardens, which had all the flowers a flower scientist could ever dream of classifying in her notebook.

"Wedding, funeral—either way, it's too far for delivery, which we don't offer anyway," said Zoocheeni. "You're on your own."

Zoocheeni disappeared in a puff of smoke with their $100 bill.

Spencer apologized that he couldn't give them a ride. "I'm still saving up for that car."

Unassisted, the team raced—or rather, walked, slowly and awkwardly—home with their new magic trick.

4

The Rehearsal for the Rehearsal Brunch

Oliver couldn't imagine anyone living in the creepy splendor of the Hauntington mansion. Nearly

every room was bigger than the entire apartment
complex where Oliver lived with his mother and
thirty other families. The doors were fit for giants.
The chandeliers were the size of cars. The cobwebs
were as long and luxuriant as the drapery.

The twins had no trouble imagining such riches.

"I'd buy a dessert island," Teenie said.

"You mean a *desert* island," said Oliver.

"No. A dessert island. I'm thinking ice cream island."

"Well, I'd buy dessert for everyone in need," Bea said. "And a quill pen, because I've always wanted one."

It was the morning of the wedding. Oliver, Bea, and Teenie were rehearsing for the rehearsal brunch in the mansion's library.

A series of stern Hauntington family portraits lined the walls. Teenie circled the room, delighted to discover that the paintings kept staring at her wherever she stood.

"Can you see me now? . . . Can you see me now? . . . Can you see me now? . . . Look—they're still watching me!"

Bea kept busy pulling books from the shelves "in order to read and look for secret passages."

Benny, who'd only come grudgingly to the wedding, was rehearsing with Oliver. Or he was supposed to be.

Unlike the girls, Benny was not a fan of the Hauntington mansion or its

I WAS SURE IT WOULD BE **S** FOR **SECRET**! BUT NOTHING'S MOVING!

artwork. "Those paintings keep following me!" he complained. "Can't you turn them around?"

"Don't you like *that* painting?" Oliver asked. "She has a pet rabbit."

"That's not a pet rabbit!" Benny yelped. "That's a rabbit stole. How would you like to be made into a fur stole?"

"But I don't have any fur."

"Well, better not get any ideas looking at mine!"

Upon closer inspection, the rabbit in the painting did look more like an accessory than a pet.

Obviously, Oliver and Benny could not turn the paintings around, so they compromised by turning themselves around.

They hid behind a potted plant and practiced a new card trick.

The trick was a bit too tricky for Oliver.

"How am I supposed to do a false shuffle? I can barely do a real shuffle!"

"Don't worry," Bea reassured him. "You've got plenty of time. Uncle Jeff is still giving his speech, and he takes forever."

From one of the bay windows, they could see the terrace where the twins' uncle Jeff was telling a very long—and knowing Uncle Jeff, very inappropriate—story.

"And once he gets done, we still have to introduce you," Bea added. "Our introduction is really long."

"We practiced all night," Teenie said. "I'd say you have about an hour left."

Just as Oliver started to calm down, a series of burps shook the window.

"Oh, no!" Bea exclaimed.

"What?!"

"The burps. That's his big closer!"

They all leaned against the window to listen. Oliver wasn't certain, but the burps sounded a little like Beethoven.

"Thank you, Jeff. That was really . . . from the gut." Miguel removed his handkerchief and wiped the microphone before handing it to his groom-to-be, Simon, who refused to touch it.

"I'll just project," Simon said, fiddling with his worm-patterned tie. "Can everyone hear me? A degree from Yale Drama School has to be good for something."

Simon paused for laughter. Finding none, he continued:

"I hope everyone enjoyed their meal. Sorry about the hollandaise . . . We've got a special treat for you folks. Please welcome our daughters, Beatriz and Martina!"

The brunch crowd burst into applause as the girls and Oliver entered. As always in their family, Bea and Teenie stole the show.

"Are you ready to be impressed beyond your

wildest dreams?" Bea asked in the voice of a boisterous magic promoter. "Please give it up for the magical stylings of the Unbelievable Oliver and his executive assistants, the Brilliant Bea and the Magical Martina!"

"It's the Terrifying Teenie!" said Teenie. "And you were supposed to say my name first this time, but I don't really care about the order."

Everyone clapped. Except Oliver. He'd been expecting a much longer introduction.

Showtime!

Bea and Teenie beckoned Oliver to the stage, then stepped away, leaving him alone with the mic and an audience of about forty confused brunch guests.

"Thank you, Brilliant Bea and, er, Terrible Martina," Oliver said. "And thank you Mr. Miguel and Mr. Simon for finally getting married."

Oliver gulped. He forgot how he was going to start.

"C'mon, you're a magician," Benny whispered in his ear. "Keep up the patter. Ask for a volunteer if you're stuck."

"I need a magician," declared Oliver, flustered. "Do I have a magician in the audience? Er, a volunteer. A magician's volunteer!"

Oliver looked out at the tables. The wedding guests were beginning to talk among themselves. His mother sat near the front. She emptied her glass and raised her hand for another.

"Oh, don't look at me," Oliver's mother said. "I'm not volunteering for anything. I'm on vacation."

"Call up Dad," said Teenie in a loud whisper.

"Oh, right." Oliver pointed at Simon, who had not raised his hand. "We have a volunteer! Mr. Dad, *er*, Simon. Please make your way to the stage."

The crowd clapped as Simon made his way onto the terrace.

"Now, Mr. Simon, we don't know each other, do we?" asked Oliver.

"You come to our house every day after school," said Simon.

"True," said Oliver. "But we don't know what each other is thinking."

Simon looked at him askance. "What *are* you thinking?"

"Even though we've only just met, I can read your mind," Oliver said. "My assistant will hand you a book. Open it to any page and write down the first word you see."

Bea handed her father an encyclopedia volume. He flipped through the pages, then wrote down a word on the sticky note attached to the dust jacket.

"I couldn't see." Oliver turned to the crowd. "Did he write a word? Good. Now, Mr. Simon, crumple the note so I still can't see it, and place it in your back pocket. Then hand the book back to me."

Simon hid the note, then handed the book to Oliver, who immediately flipped through the pages, rather obviously checking the jacket of the book.

"Bea!" Oliver called in a panic. She tiptoed over so they could talk without the audience hearing. "Bea, this isn't the right book. This is *K*. You were supposed to give him *J*."

"Oh, *J* was boring," Bea said. "The sequel's much better."

Oliver hit his head with the "sequel." He'd hidden a piece of carbon paper in the first book, so that when Simon wrote down his word, it would appear on another piece of paper, also hidden in the book. Now Oliver had no idea what word Simon had chosen.

Carbon copy of volunteer's word.

"Okay, I noticed you were looking near the front of the book? Right?"

Oliver flipped through the book, hoping that a word would catch his eye. He considered his odds. What was the most commonly used word?

"Was it, um, *the*? Is *the* your word?"

Simon was confused. His actual word was *karma*.

He glanced over at his daughters, who both looked meaningfully at him.

"Yes," Simon said. "My word was *the*. How'd you know?"

Oliver beamed. He'd done it—real magic!

"A magician never reveals his secrets!" To keep up the momentum, he rushed right into his big trick. "And now for the grand finale. Teenie? Bea?"

The girls rushed Simon off the terrace and into the library. From the other side of the wall Simon could be heard saying, "You want me to get in *that*? Wearing *these* shoes?"

"I'll need one more volunteer." Oliver scanned the crowd.

A few hands went up. But he pointed to the other groom, Miguel, who had his camera pointed at Oliver. (Miguel had chosen to save money by photographing his own wedding.)

"Mr. Miguel!"

Miguel shook his head. He didn't want to volunteer. But the crowd clapped and cheered until

Miguel reluctantly handed his camera to Spencer and joined Oliver on the terrace stage.

Spencer shot enough photos to blind everyone with the flash.

"Hello," said Oliver. "What's your name, sir?"

"Now, Oliver—"

"That's my name too!"

As the crowd laughed, Oliver gained confidence. Perhaps too much confidence. "Well, Mr. Oliver, what brings you to Hauntington Gardens today?"

"It's Mr. Miguel. I mean, it's Miguel. Just Miguel. I'm getting married. This is our rehearsal brunch."

"Oh, a wedding and a brunch!" Oliver improvised. "A day when two become one. And a meal where two meals become one. Breakfast and lunch . . . But for my next trick, one will become two."

He waved his wand, the signal for the twins to reappear with the coffin and dolly. But they were having technical difficulties.

"Dad, we need you to be quiet and not make a

scene," Teenie told Simon. "Like how we're supposed to act at nice restaurants."

As they rolled the coffin onto the terrace, a sharp-eared audience member might have heard some unexpected sounds coming from inside it.

With everyone in place, Oliver turned to Miguel. "Please, sir, step into the coffin."

"Do I have to?" asked Miguel, looking at his watch. "Simon and I have to do our portraits soon. Where is he, by the way?"

"I promise it's perfectly safe," said Oliver, avoiding Miguel's question. "Nothing to fear but the worms. And spiders," he added, indicating Miguel's spider-patterned tie.

He lifted the lid and helped Miguel inside. Now both grooms were tucked into the Sawed in Half. Bea reached in and pulled Simon's feet out of the far side to match Miguel's head and arms, which were sticking out the front.

"Teenie, the saw, please."

"Ow!" Teenie pretended to hurt her finger on the plastic saw. The audience gasped.

Grinning, she showed everyone that her finger was fine, and handed the saw to Oliver.

"Thank you, Terrifying Teenie—that really was terrifying. And now, I'm sorry to say, we must saw your father in half."

With the saw in hand, Oliver made a show of trying to cut through the center of the coffin. He quickly turned to the two assistants.

"On second thought, you guys should do this. He's your father."

Enjoying it more than they should have, the girls took turns sawing through the coffin.

He played his part well, screaming just enough to make the gag work.

"Well done," said Oliver after the saw had gone all the way through. "Let's just make sure the bones are fully separated . . ."

The three kids started to separate the two halves of the coffin. "Oh no, there's too much blood!" said Oliver, stopping them. "Towels, please."

The girls placed towels over the "cut" ends of each half of the coffin, so it would seem they were hiding the bloody parts. Then they pushed the two coffin halves away from each other and turned them toward the audience.

"And voila!" Oliver said. "Mr. Papa is sawed in half!"

Miguel tilted his head so he could see Simon's feet sticking out of the other box. "Why are my feet still wiggling?" he asked. "And why am I wearing Simon's socks?"

The audience clapped. Oliver reflexively bowed and moved to leave the stage.

"Kid, you gotta put him back together," Benny whispered. "Don't want people to worry."

"Oops!" said Oliver aloud.

The audience thought it was all part of the act, and laughed along as Oliver turned and moved the two halves of the coffin back together. He tapped the coffin twice with his wand, then opened the front lid.

Miguel emerged to universal applause. The twins hastily pushed Simon's feet back inside, lest the illusion be spoiled.

"Thank you, thank you!" Oliver said as he accepted a flower thrown to the stage.

"Hey, those are for decoration!" Miguel shouted. (In addition to photographing the wedding, he was also the florist.) "But bravo, Oliver, Bea, and Teenie! Let's hear it for the Unbelievable Oliver and his Uncanny Assistants."

That went pretty well, all things considered, Oliver thought as they wheeled the coffin back into the library.

What Did We Forget?

Worn out from the performance, the twins and Oliver relaxed in the library.

Bea sat on the coffin, looking at her notebook, but not writing anything. Teenie jumped up and down on an ottoman, causing clouds of dust to form. Oliver practiced palming a coin—almost successfully. Benny napped on the sofa beside him.

"I feel like I forgot something, but I don't know what it is," said Bea, drumming her fingers on the coffin.

"Me too," said Teenie. "Oh, I know! We didn't use our new names! The Busy Bea and the Thrilling Teenie."

"No. It was something else, and those aren't our names. What did we forget? I can't put my finger on it."

"Then it must not have been important," said Oliver. "Don't worry about it."

Bea looked at him in amazement. "Did you just say 'Don't worry about it'? Wow. I don't think I've ever seen you not nervous before."

"Sawing people in half really agrees with you, Oliver," Teenie said.

"Really? You think so?" Nervous at the thought of being un-nervous, Oliver dropped his coin to the floor. "Now that you mention it, *I* feel like we forgot something, too."

Miguel entered with hands full of flowers and cameras. His neck craned, he talked on the phone.

"What do you mean it's too big to fit through the door? We ordered a sensible, five-tiered cake— Zesty Orange, Ritzy Raspberry, Strawberry Angel Food, Very Vanilla, and I-forget-what Chocolate, topped with Butterscotch Buttercream and Galaxy Ganache. Now it's *ten* tiers? With carrot cake?!"

The twins looked at each other. "I thought it was supposed to be Choco-latte Ganache," whispered Bea.

Teenie shook her head. "No. Lucky Lemon. I'm sure of it."

"What? No, there is no wedding planner," Miguel shouted into his phone. "Well, you're talking with one of them. I don't know where the other one went.

"Kids, have you seen your dad, um, Mr. Simon?"

Miguel asked. "He was supposed to check on the cake when it arrived."

"We'll check on the cake for you, Mr. Miguel." Oliver jumped up, glad to have a job now that relaxing was no longer relaxing. "You just, um, take it easy and handle the flowers. And the photos. And the guests."

The kids found the baker in the kitchen, wiping his brow with one of the many tea towels he carried in the band of his apron.

"Oh, hello, children!" Jacques said. "Did you see the beautiful cake? A caterer just helped me get it into the fridge . . ."

Jacques showed them the walk-in refrigerator. Inside was a multitiered, multicolored cake so tall and unwieldy that it was placed on wheels.

This was the biggest, most glorious dessert any of the children had ever seen.

"The top five tiers are on the house," said the baker proudly. "I decided you were such a sweet family, you deserved the biggest and sweetest of cakes."

"You are a true artist, sir," said Oliver.

The cake was so well constructed that Oliver felt an overwhelming desire to shake the man's hand.

Their hands met with a poof of flour and powdered sugar.

"I'll be returning to help serve the cake later," said the baker. "When you see Simon, please tell him."

The kids looked at one another. Simon—that's what they'd forgotten! They'd forgotten to let him out of the sawed-in-half trick.

"Daddy's stuck in the coffin!" Bea whispered, horrified.

The three of them dashed back to the library.

"Daddy?" Teenie knocked on the lid of the coffin. "We're so, so sorry. I promise never to leave you in a coffin again."

"Me too," said Bea. "Well, at least until you die, I guess?"

Oliver lifted the lid. The coffin was empty.

Define Missing

Oliver gulped. He'd never lost a parent before. He'd lost many homework assignments. And before improving his laundry skills, he'd lost several socks. But never a parent. Or any person at all.

"Do you think he's *missing* missing?" Oliver asked. "Or just missing?"

"Define *missing*," Teenie said. "He's probably just run off."

Bea nodded. "He gets restless. Parents these days don't have nearly the freedom they used to."

"He's fine without supervision," Teenie agreed. "Usually."

"As long as he doesn't park in a big parking lot," said Bea.

"He loses his car a lot," Teenie explained.

"But it's not like he loses *himself*," Bea specified.

Benny had hopped over from the sofa as soon as the coffin was revealed to be empty. "Psst." He nudged Oliver, who picked him up in the top hat.

"Maybe their dad got wise," whispered the rabbit. "Better to leave early than to get left at the altar. Believe me."

"You mean you think he *left* left?" Oliver whispered back, scandalized. "But he wouldn't . . . would he?"

"Anyway," said Bea, too distracted to notice that her friend was conferring with a rabbit, "Dad always has his phone."

"Actually, *we* have his phone, remember?" Teenie held up their father's phone.

"Oh, right," said Bea. "The gift for Daddy and Papa."

Oliver was confused. "Your having his phone is a gift for *them*?"

"Yes, the gift of time away from technology," said Teenie. "To make the day special." She put the phone down on a table.

"Also, we're making a wedding video," said Bea. "That's our real present."

"That's right," said Teenie. "And Oliver, we need your help."

Normally, Miguel shot all the family videos. But considering he was already doing the flowers and the still photography, the girls had volunteered—as long as they got to use Simon's phone. (They swore they wouldn't open any apps until after the wedding ceremony.)

Oliver had been the victim of several of Bea and Teenie's previous videos.

He hoped this video would be less hazardous. In fact, he hoped he wouldn't be involved in it at all.

"Maybe I should go look for Mr. Simon instead," said Oliver.

Simon's phone buzzed on the table.

"I think your dad has a text." Oliver waited for the girls to pick it up. "It might be important."

"Our dad never does anything important," said Teenie. "He's a writer."

Teenie handed Oliver a stick with a single ear bud taped to it. "Here's your boom pole. You're running sound."

"Teenie is the cinematographer," Bea explained. "I'm doing the on-camera interviews."

She pulled out her notebook. "Oliver, do you have anything to say to the groom and groom?"

Teenie turned the phone to face Oliver. Apparently, they were starting right away.

"See, that wasn't so hard." Bea made a check-mark in her notebook. "Now we just have to interview a hundred fifty more guests."

"I don't know what you're congratulating them for," Benny whispered into Oliver's ear. "There isn't going to be a wedding if the groom doesn't show."

"Let's start with family members," said Bea. This made sense, as only family members were around at the moment.

Surrounded by crates, Uncle Jeff was moving bottles behind the bar.

He shook his head as soon as he heard the word *interview*.

"I had a job interview once. Let's just say it didn't go well. Besides, there's something I want you to help me out with."

All the crates looked too heavy for the kids to lift, and the contents didn't look safe for kids.

"Oh, not the bar. I just need you to pull my finger real quick."

The twins were far too smart for such a trick, but

Oliver reached out his hand and pulled Uncle Jeff's finger.

The fart sound wouldn't have been so loud if Oliver hadn't had the microphone extended as well.

"You kids catch that on video?" Uncle Jeff laughed. "Hey, tell your dads the bar's all set up. If they need anything, I'll be right here."

They found Simon's sister on the back steps of the mansion, leaning against a snarling stone lion.

Aunt Margie was a favorite of the twins. She always brought them souvenirs from her travels, or "mystical journeys," as she called them. And she was always careful to tell the girls which items had the most magic powers.

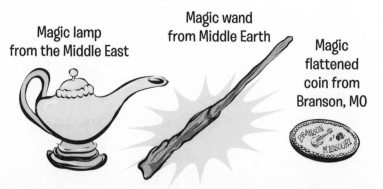

Magic lamp from the Middle East

Magic wand from Middle Earth

Magic flattened coin from Branson, MO

"Hello, Bea and Teenie! Have you seen your dad?" she asked.

"No," said Bea quickly. "Can we interview you for our video?"

"Of course! I was just working on the wedding ceremony."

She held up a notebook and a quill pen, just like the one Bea wanted. Bea made a mental note to ask her aunt for a pen as a gift for the Winter Solstice, which is how Aunt Margie celebrated Christmas.

Ordained in seven faiths, she was the obvious choice to officiate her brother's wedding.

"Now, the first thing to know about Simon is that he's a restless soul . . ."

Aunt Margie launched into a long discussion of their father's character, starting with his star sign (Libra) and favorite animal (llama).

"He never sticks with anything for long. He once promised to travel with me around the world for a year, but didn't last a week. So fickle! I'm surprised he's stayed with Miguel all this time. And now they're getting married? He'll run off at the first—"

She noticed her nieces' expressions. "Of course, he's probably changed. I'm sure I missed something in his star chart."

Teenie's hands were getting tired from holding the camera. Oliver's arm had fallen asleep from lifting the boom.

Bea did her best to get her aunt to wrap it up. "That's nice, Aunt Margie. In five words or less, what would you like to wish the happy couple?"

With that their aunt put her hands together and bowed for the camera.

As they started off in search of their next interview subject, Miguel approached. He held what looked like a fence dotted with donuts.

Teenie trained the phone camera on him.

"If you see Dad, remind him that he was in charge of the donut wall," said Miguel, waving the camera away. "It was his idea. I don't even eat donuts!"

"We do!" They each stole a donut as he walked by. Even Benny stuck a paw out of the top hat and snatched one.

Luckily, the wall blocked Miguel's view of their thievery.

As she nibbled on her donut (plain glazed), Bea wrote down what Miguel had said. So far, most of her notes were things Simon was supposed to do that he wasn't doing.

"Dad really is dropping the ball," she said.

"He's not dropping the ball, he's dropping the wedding," Benny (maple bar) told Oliver (strawberry cruller).

Oliver was about to shush Benny when he heard a buzzing sound.

"I think your dad's phone is buzzing," he said.

"Uh-huh." Teenie nodded. She made no move to look at it, or even touch it. She was still eating her donut (chocolate sprinkles).

"What if it's him?" suggested Oliver. "What if he really is missing?"

"I think I liked you better when you were in your not-nervous phase," said Bea. "You should try being not nervous again."

The phone kept buzzing. Oliver kept trying not to be nervous about it.

"Oh, fine," said Teenie. "We can look at the phone. Just to make you happy."

She took the phone out of her pocket and glanced at the screen. Her glance turned into a stare.

"Dad's going to Mexico!"

"Mexico?!" Benny exclaimed in alarm. Oliver could feel the rabbit's feet scrambling around on his head, and then the hat being lifted. "I knew it!"

"What?" asked Oliver.

"Weddings—they're all alike!" said the rabbit, jumping to the ground. "I should never have come!"

Before Oliver could ask Benny what he was talking about, he'd hopped out of sight.

Runaways

In a rush, the twins declared two things:

First, their father was not allowed to go to Mexico without them.

"It's not fair," said Teenie. "He knows we've always wanted to go!"

"He can go to Canada," said Bea. "Maybe."

Second, Oliver was not allowed to run after his runaway rabbit—not when they had a runaway father to contend with.

"Rabbits are cute, but you have to admit they're easier to replace," said Bea. "I mean, you can't get a new dad at a pet store."

"That's right," said her sister. "We need your help catching Dad before he disappears forever!"

Luckily, they knew somebody who was an expert at catching fugitives.

Grandpa Bruce was a retired police officer. They found him pacing around the grand entry hall, where a pile of gifts had already started to grow.

"Amazing the way folks leave their presents out in the open like that," he grumbled. "Think you can trust people just because they're invited guests? Half of this junk will be gone in an hour! Now what's this video you're making? I hope it's for the insurance claim."

His granddaughters told him about the wedding video, and asked if they could interview him.

"Let me give you some advice about interviews," Grandpa Bruce said. "Don't ever let your subject know what you know or don't know. And don't ask permission. Just start asking questions."

"Okay," said Bea. "Say someone ran away, how would you catch them?"

"Heh. This is my kind of wedding video. Nothing lovey-dovey. Straight to the important stuff. Well, the sad truth is, you often don't catch them unless they want to be caught."

The kids looked at one another. This was not encouraging.

"Did our dad run away before?" asked Teenie. "I mean, *ever*. Like when he was a kid."

"Not that I recall. We were always much more worried about him being kidnapped, really. Always with his head in the clouds, your dad. And so gullible."

"Kidnapped?" the kids repeated in unison.

Grandpa Bruce nodded. "Your grandmother, god rest her soul, kept a drawer full of money, just in case we needed to pay a ransom. Those bills wound up coming in handy, let me tell you, when it was time to pay for college."

After the interview, the kids pondered what Grandpa Bruce had said. Could Simon have been kidnapped? They hadn't even considered the possibility until now.

"Kidnappers usually leave a note," said Bea, tapping her nose with her pen.

"Yeah, they make those cool collages out of magazines," said Teenie.

The kids saw plenty of notes around the gift table. There was even a bird cage filled with greeting cards.

The twins looked through the cards, gingerly avoiding the bird, who looked ill-tempered.

Oliver checked the guest book.

CONGRATS SIMON + MIGUEL!
— SPENCER
P.S. WAY TO GO!

D + ♡ + 3⅗ ♡ Margie

Guest Book

TO THE FAMILY:
ROSES ARE RED.
DOVES ARE GRAY
TO SEE HIM AGAIN
YOU'LL HAVE TO PAY

"Oh, that's nice," said Oliver. "There's a poet in the family."

"You got a funny idea of nice," Benny said.

Benny's right, thought Oliver. "It's a ransom poem!"

The twins were not impressed.

"There's no such thing as a ransom poem, Oliver," said Teenie confidently.

She held up an envelope. "Isn't this cool? It has our names on it! Not just our dads', or For the Family."

"Well, aren't you going to open it?" asked Oliver.

"No, you don't open presents until after the wedding ceremony," said Bea. "And before the cake. Everyone knows that, Oliver."

With this key point of etiquette established, there was no more to be learned at the gift table. They decided to go back to the scene of the crime.

The library was just the way they'd left it. Nothing seemed amiss.

They spun the coffin in all directions. If anything, it was in better shape than before. The wheels spun more smoothly and hardly made any noise. Maybe it was lighter without their fathers inside.

"Seems fine to me," Teenie said, standing on the coffin. "Somebody give me a push."

Teenie was starting to pick up speed when the dolly hit something at the edge of the landing. The coffin tipped over and she slid off.

"Aaack! What was that?!" said Teenie, stumbling to her feet.

It was just a pair of shoes. Their dad's shoes. She pushed them aside.

"Well, nothing's different around here. No signs of foul play."

"I figured dad-napping was a stretch." Bea wrote a note in her notebook. "He must have run away to Mexico after all."

"What about his shoes?" Oliver gestured to Simon's shoes, now lying upside down.

"What about them? He took them off to get in the coffin, remember?"

"Yeah, but wouldn't he put them back on?"

"I'm sure they sell shoes in Mexico, Oliver. But I see your point," Bea admitted.

The three investigators were silent for a moment.

"Parents are always making you put your shoes on when you go outside," said Teenie finally. "Why? I never understood it."

Simon's phone buzzed again. This time Teenie looked at it immediately. "Oh no!"

"What?!"

"I don't think Dad went to Mexico after all."

Their investigation had taken a terrible turn.

The text could not have been clearer, regardless of what the letters looked like. Even Teenie had to agree.

Their father had been kidnapped, and the kidnapper would be returning later to collect the ransom money.

"Shouldn't they have said how much the ransom was?" said Bea. "They must not be very experienced kidnappers."

> **MESSAGE**
>
> The item is safe n sound in cold storage. I'll be back later. Have money ready.

"What does it matter? We don't have any money anyway," Teenie pointed out.

"True," reflected Bea. "Maybe we could offer something in trade."

"Like what?" asked Oliver, who was getting more and more distressed.

The twins looked at him, considering. He gulped.

9

Hostage Negotiations

If there was anyone who could help with a financial negotiation it was Miguel's parents, who were partners in a small law firm in Tucson.

Of course, the kids didn't want to raise the alarm about the dad-napping; they would have to be sneaky in their line of questioning.

FAMILY LAW: GETTING MARRIED? DIVORCED? TERMINALLY ILL?

Montoya and Montoya

WE CAN HELP.

"Lita and Lito, will you be in our video?" Bea asked her grandparents.

Miguel encouraged his children to use Spanish when referring to his parents. So the twins called their grandmother and grandfather Abuelita and Abuelito, affectionately shortened to Lita and Lito.

Both were working hard, preparing for the ceremony. Their grandfather was in charge of assembling the wedding canopy, which looked as though it was about to fall down.

Lita, meanwhile, was placing paper flowers around the stage.

The twins' grandmother had constructed more than a hundred flowers in all shapes and sizes. Some were as big as Bea and Teenie. They were beautiful and must have taken days to make.

"Oh, are you filming already?" their grandmother asked, addressing the camera. "Miguel and Simon, we love you both so much. I just wish you'd told me you were also using real flowers before I made so many paper ones."

"And it wouldn't hurt to have instructions for this chuppah you ordered from Sweden!" said their grandfather jovially.

Lita nudged Lito. "Say something nice."

"Yes, yes, we couldn't be happier to have Simon as our son-in-law. And, hey, if it doesn't work out, we can always handle the divorce! Congratulations, guys!"

"I have a question that I think my dads would want to know the answer to," said Teenie. "Do you have any experience with kidnappings?"

"Or hostage negotiations of any kind?" added Bea.

Their grandfather laughed. "Why, are you planning on being kidnapped?"

"Not exactly," said Bea. "We're just trying to

prepare them for all the different things that could happen to a married couple."

Miguel's parents admitted they had little experience with kidnappers. But they had one piece of advice: Learn all you can about them.

"Find out what they're really after," said their grandfather. "You don't want to pay a ransom if they're not going to give you back your loved one anyway."

"And remember, you always have two lawyers to lean on," said their grandmother.

The twins thanked their grandparents for a lovely interview.

After a whispered consultation, they decided they should check the front entrance of the gardens. If they knew who'd entered and exited the property, they might have a better idea as to the identity of the kidnapper.

Spencer, wearing a valet uniform, was standing in the circular driveway. He was more than happy to be interviewed for their video, seeing as he wasn't doing anything except waiting for guests to arrive.

"What about people leaving?" asked Teenie. "Have you seen any runaway grooms?"

Spencer laughed. "Why? Are your dads getting cold feet?"

"Why did you say that?" asked Bea sharply. "Did you see a pair of feet?"

"No. It's just an expression."

"And what about suspicious-looking objects?" pressed Teenie. "Something human-size maybe, like a mummy? Or anything with arms and legs sticking out?"

"No, nothing like that," said Spencer. "Nobody has come or gone for an hour. Not since the baker left and the caterers arrived."

"Really? Nobody at all?" The kids looked at one another in surprise. "Is there another way out?"

"Nope. This place is like a walled fortress." Spencer eyed the phone in Teenie's hand. "I like this video you're making. It's kind of *Simon and Miguel's Wedding: American Crime Story*."

"Excuse me, can you tell us where to find the corpse flower?"

A pair of tourists were walking up, cameras and guidebooks in hand.

"Sorry, the gardens are closed for a special event," said Spencer. "But I'm sure—"

Before Spencer could finish, a tall, frowning man in dirty gardener's overalls and a fraying straw hat stepped in front of the tourists.

"The corpse flower does not like visitors," he said in such an unfriendly voice that the tourists backed away without another word.

The grim-faced gardener nodded curtly, then disappeared as silently as he'd come.

Bea pulled the video crew away from Spencer.

"Nobody has left the premises," she said, tapping her notebook. "That means Dad didn't run away AND the kidnapper didn't take him away."

"So then he's here," said Oliver. "Which is good news, right?"

Teenie nodded. "I mean, so what if he's a prisoner? What could happen to him at good old Hauntington Gardens?"

They all turned to take in the view. From where they stood in the shadow of the old stone mansion, they could see the cobwebby conservatory in which the famously foul-smelling corpse flower bloomed. It was not a reassuring sight.

The gardener was standing in front of the conservatory and appeared to be communicating with the flower inside.

"I wonder why they call them corpse flowers," said Teenie.

"I thought it was because they smell like corpses," said Oliver.

"Yeah, but *why* do they smell like that?" asked Teenie darkly.

As they watched, the gardener strode off in the direction of the giant hedge maze that bordered the gardens like a topiary fortress.

"He's going into the maze—like that monster in the Greek myth."

The twins had recently read the myth of the Minotaur, the bull-headed monster that haunted the labyrinth in ancient Crete.

"He's scarier than a Minotaur," exclaimed Bea. "He's the Garden-o-taur!"

"Wait, what if somebody else is in there?" said Teenie.

"Like Dad?"

Teenie nodded. If Simon was lost, which seemed more than likely, knowing him, the hedge maze was the logical place to look for him. After all, it was designed to get lost in.

A cloud passed in front of the sun, casting dark shadows over the gardens and causing the kids to shiver.

"Okay, Teenie, you better go in to look for him," said Bea grimly.

"But I just did a maze this morning!"

"That maze was on paper. It doesn't count."

"It's okay," said Oliver bravely. "I'll go."

"You will?" The twins stared at him in surprise.

"I have to. The Garden-o-taur is chasing Benny!"

Oliver pointed to the small white animal running into the hedge maze with the very large gardener chasing after him.

"I hope he doesn't feed Benny to the corpse flower!" said Teenie. "We'll come too!"

Rabbit Run

Benny couldn't believe his luck. The vegetable patch at Hauntington Gardens was laid out like a buffet, with each dish carefully labeled and presented. "Better than brunch at the Sands," Benny said to himself, fondly remembering the buffets at his favorite Las Vegas casino.

However, just like in Vegas, Benny's luck ran out. The Hauntington Gardens' gardener had caught him chewing on some parsnip, and had chased him into the hedge maze. Benny was still a few feet ahead of his pursuer, but he was lost. If he didn't find his way out of the maze soon, he'd be swept up in the gardener's net.

Worse yet, a rat blocked his way. Benny hated rats. They always got other, more respectable rodents into trouble.

"Outta my way, rat," Benny said.

"What are you running from, mate?" the rat asked. "Bunch of pesky kids back that way."

"I'm running from the gardener."

"Oh, he's harmless, unless you're a topiary," the rat said. "It's the chef you've got to worry about. She'll dice you to bits and feed you to the guests. And you're headed right for her kitchen. Trust me, nobody knows this maze better than me."

Benny didn't trust rats, but he didn't trust chefs either. He asked which way to go.

IT'S SIMPLE. JUST LEFT, RIGHT, LEFT AT THE HEDGE, ANOTHER LEFT AT THE SHRUB, A RIGHT AT THE BUSH, PAST THE TOPIARY, THEN JUST CRAWL UNDER THE SCRUB.

Benny soon discovered he'd been right not to trust the rat. Sure, the rat led him out of the maze— straight into the most terrifying area.

The wedding.

Guests were everywhere now, along with servers passing appetizers from the dreaded kitchen. One wrong step and he'd be turned into a canapé.

To make matters worse, the gardener was approaching with his net.

Sitting at the bar was the one person Benny could trust at this wedding other than Oliver: Diane, Oliver's mother.

Benny jumped into Diane's lap just as the gardener swung for him with his net.

"Ma'am, watch out for that rabbit!"

"Don't be silly, this is my rabbit," said Diane. "Well, my son's rabbit."

"Sorry, we don't allow animals off leash at the Hauntington," said the gardener. "Not even rabbits."

"He's a service rabbit." Diane stroked Benny's head. "Surely you make exceptions for service rabbits. Doctor's orders. I'm a registered nurse. Here, we have all the paperwork somewhere."

Diane opened her purse and pulled out a stethoscope, some tissues, and various snacks.

"No, that's fine, ma'am," said the gardener kindly. "We just can't have him in the gardens. If you like, we have a petting zoo for rabbits, goats, and geese."

Benny yelped in horror.

"No, but thank you," said Diane as the gardener walked away, shaking his head in puzzlement.

Oliver's mother wagged her finger at Benny. "You know not to go running away like that."

SORRY, DIANE.

She stared at the rabbit, then noticed Uncle Jeff standing behind the bar.

"Oh, phew. You're still here. For a second I thought I heard the rabbit talking!"

Uncle Jeff smiled and placed a crudité platter in front of her. "Hungry?"

"No, but I'm sure he is." Diane swung Benny onto the bar. He immediately started nibbling. Even though he was beyond full, a little bit of celery couldn't hurt.

"Man, am I tired!" Diane yawned as Uncle Jeff started rinsing glasses. "I haven't slept in days. Oh, the life of an ER nurse."

His mouth full of broccoli and carrots, Benny tried his best to make polite conversation. "Sounds like show business. Long hours, late nights. You don't choose the life, it chooses you."

"Cheers to that," Diane said.

She clinked glasses with a confused Uncle Jeff, who was drying a wet glass with a rag. He shrugged and ducked below the bar.

"I wanted a quiet life," Benny continued. "A little burrow in the country. Twenty . . . thirty kids max. But Daisy had to have a big wedding. So we go to Vegas. What happens? She runs off with some high-rolling hare and leaves me at the altar!"

"That's such a sad story, Jeff," said Diane, still

thinking it was the bartender talking. "But honestly, twenty kids is too many for anybody."

"Sure is," said Jeff, standing again. As far as he was concerned, one kid was too many.

Benny finished the last of the carrots and crawled into Oliver's mother's lap. Maybe she'd have more snacks. Moms often carried snacks.

From Maze to Mansion

Teenie led the way through the hedge maze, holding her father's phone in front of her, so as to check around corners and avoid dead ends. If they were going to die in the maze, she wanted to have a little warning first.

"Daddy? Are you there?" Teenie called out.

Bea followed behind, at a safe-ish distance. "Daddy, if you hear us, send up a flare!"

Oliver was last. "Benny? Can you hear me?"

"Here, Benny, Benny, Benny!" called Teenie.

"Shh!" said Oliver. "He hates that!"

Turning and turning, going deeper and deeper

into the maze, they didn't find any lost fathers or lost rabbits.

Instead, *they* got lost.

Sadly, characters in books don't have an all-seeing, bird's-eye view of their surroundings. Happily, we authors and readers do. *We* can't get lost.

"I wish we had a ladder to see over that hedge," said Oliver.

Without warning, Teenie jumped on Bea's shoulders. She couldn't see the exit.

But she could see something else. "It's the Garden-o-taur! Run!"

WAIT UP!

Teenie grabbed handfuls of petals to toss behind them as they ran.

"Don't worry, Oliver," Teenie shouted. "I'm a trained flower assassin, just follow the petals!"

Oliver followed the trail and got stuck in the same dead ends as Teenie and Bea.

With each wrong turn, he could hear the gardener getting closer.

SNIP. SNIP. SNIP.

Finally, Bea couldn't take it any longer. "That's it! I'm breaking out!" The trail of flower petals ended in a girl-shaped hole in the hedge.

Oliver slipped through the hole and found himself sliding down a slimy staircase that ended underneath the mansion.

"Aaack!" He crashed through an open door and landed in a heap at the bottom of the stairs, which would have been even more painful had not the twins been there to break his fall.

It was almost too dark to see, with the only light coming from the door they'd entered, but at least they were together again.

"Do you think this is the dungeon?" Bea said. "A mansion this size must have at least one dungeon."

"What else could it be?" Teenie said.

Bea didn't see any wall shackles or other standard dungeon décor. But there were a great many barrels. She'd read enough horror stories to know that any one of them could be housing their father.

She tapped on a barrel. "Maybe they're hiding Dad in here." Something scampered out of the top, but it wasn't their father.

"What was that?!" asked Oliver.

Teenie used her father's phone to light the room. There was a single well-fed raccoon in the corner, shielding its eyes.

"Oh, don't worry," said Teenie. "It's just a raccoon."

"AAAHHH!" Bea and Oliver were both properly scared of raccoons.

The raccoon looked at them disdainfully, then wandered away.

"Where's the light switch?" said Oliver.

He felt around on the wall but found only holes.

"Maybe there's a string or something you pull?" suggested Bea.

"I don't want to check the ceiling," said Oliver. "What if there are bats up there?"

Teenie flashed the phone's light overhead.

"See, almost no bats!"

But there were many cobwebs and a single rope. When they pulled it, a trapdoor opened, and a ladder dropped to the floor with a clang.

Secret Passages

The ladder led back into the library.

"I knew there was a secret passage!" Bea shouted before remembering that she was in a library. "I just didn't check enough books to find the secret lever," she added in an appropriate whisper.

A book stuck out from the shelf. It was the slim *Y* volume of the encyclopedia. (Bea had previously stopped at *X*.) She pushed the book back into place, and the trapdoor in the floor slammed shut.

The library grew quiet, even for a library.

"Do you hear that?" Teenie whispered. "Someone's talking on the other side of this shelf. There must be a secret room!"

"Another one?" said Bea skeptically.

"The other one was a secret staircase. The room part wasn't secret."

As the twins argued, Oliver noticed something wrong with the eyes of a painting, the painting with the rabbit fur stole.

What was wrong was that the eyes were gone.

Oliver gulped. "Maybe that's why it looked like the eyes were watching us before! Someone really *was* watching us!"

Teenie and Bea had been to enough museums with their fathers to know that you never touch the art. So, even though the portrait was suspicious, they didn't want to touch it. Oliver's mother had no time to take him to museums. He pushed on the frame without hesitation. Or none beyond his usual fear of the unknown.

As the painting turned on a hinge, a voice rang out from the other side:

"Simon, do you promise to be kind to Miguel even when you're hungry and your blood sugar is low?"

The voice was addressing their missing father. They'd solved the case in record time.

Smiling, the kids pushed through the painting and entered a new, even creepier room.

The walls were lined with animal heads, including one jackalope that looked very much like Benny would look if you stuck a pair of stag's horns on him. Oliver was glad Benny wasn't there to see it.

A second door opened into a large marble bathroom. In front of the mirror stood their aunt Margie. Pushing up her colorful reading glasses, she read from her notebook.

"And do you, Miguel, promise to stand by Simon even when the line for a theme park ride is three hours long?"

"Aunt Margie," Teenie said. "Where are you hiding Dad?"

"I'm not hiding him. Is he hidden?"

"But you were just talking to him."

"Oh, no," she said. "I'm just practicing for the ceremony."

She showed Bea her notebook, in which she'd written her script for the wedding. The notebook was gilded leather and quite elegant. Bea decided to ask for a matching notebook for Winter Solstice to go with the quill pen.

"How'd you find this room?" Teenie asked.

"Oh, it's in this brochure," their aunt Margie said. "Everyone should follow their own path, but they should also check a map."

Sure enough, when they looked at the brochure, they saw a map of the mansion. Each secret spot was marked with a spyglass.

All three kids agreed that exploring the mansion's secrets was the absolute best use of their time.

Behind the Hall of Portraits was a Hall of Secrets: secret passages and stairways that maids and butlers had used to navigate the mansion.

"Someone could have stolen Dad and dragged him anywhere!" said Bea as she climbed a spiral stairway to the seventh master bedroom.

Popping out of false walls and wardrobes, they investigated nearly every one of the house's forty rooms before finally arriving on the fourth-floor balcony.

Teenie brushed aside a "DO NOT TOUCH!" sign on a knight in once-shining armor.

"Just to see if it's heavy," said Teenie, grimacing at the weight. "It's not!"

As she lifted the armored arm, a ladder dropped to the ground. She'd found yet another hidden trapdoor.

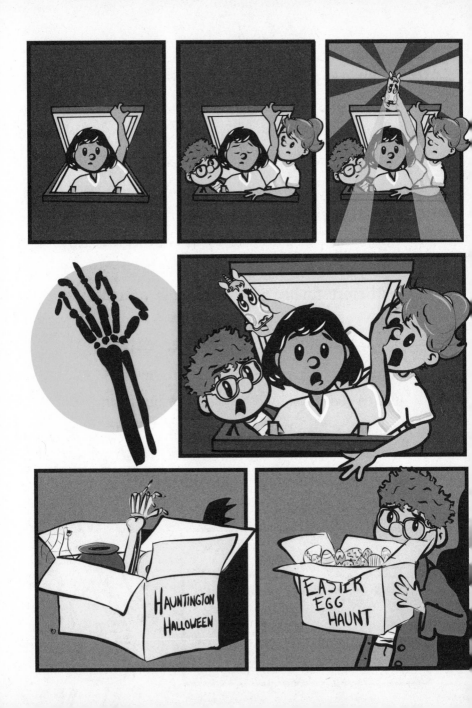

It was a lot of fun, yes, but after visiting every secret passage, closet, and hiding place, they hadn't found any grooms. Or even any ghosts.

Worse yet, from the circular window in the mansion's highest tower, they could see that most of the guests had already arrived.

Miguel, meanwhile, was perched on a ladder, hanging lights from a tree. They waved, but he couldn't see them.

The wedding was getting closer, and they were no closer to finding Simon.

Guests and Guesses

When they joined the crowd gathering for the wedding, Oliver was surprised to find Benny curled up in his mother's lap.

He never lets *me* hug him like that, Oliver thought.

Oliver wasn't so sure he wanted to hug Benny, but it would have been nice to have the option.

"I found Benny!" Oliver's mother said, nuzzling the rabbit. "The gardener was chasing you because you're a bad bunny, aren't you? Yes, you are."

She tickled Benny, who erupted in giggles. "Stop!" he begged.

"Okay, okay!" Diane said. Then she looked at her son in alarm. "Oliver, did Benny just say *Stop*?"

"No, that was me," Oliver said. "He doesn't like to be tickled or hugged or even held. He does like carrots, though."

"Well, you know him better than I do. Here, take him back." Diane handed over the disappointed rabbit.

By mutual agreement, Benny didn't stay in Oliver's arms; he went right back to his perch atop Oliver's head.

"Can we ask you a few questions?" Bea asked Oliver's mother, pulling out her notebook.

"For our wedding video," Teenie specified.

"As a parent, I wish *I* could take more naps!" said Diane. "Are you sure you don't want to hear about the time I first met your fathers?"

"We're sure," said Teenie. She turned off the camera. "Okay, that's a wrap."

The kids regrouped under the still-less-than-sturdy-but-nonetheless-stylish chuppah.

"Bea, we need a better game plan," said Teenie. "That was fine for Oliver's mom, but we can't let anyone know Dad is missing. We could cause a panic. Or even tip off the gardener or the parent-napper!"

Teenie thought for a moment. "We should ask something more subtle, like . . . 'Tell us about the first time you ever saw our dad. Now tell us about the last time you saw him.'"

"We also need a motive," Bea pointed out.

"'Why'd you steal our dad?'"

"How about, 'Tell us your fondest memory of our dad and your deepest grudge.'"

The twins tried these questions on every arriving guest. Nearly everyone said something suspicious. Many of their fathers' friends went all the way back to college and they had some very specific axes to grind.

Then there was the entire third-grade class.

The rule at Nowonder Elementary was that if an invitation went out to one student in a class, it went out to *every* student in the class. As soon as Bea and Teenie invited Oliver, the wedding became a class field trip to Hauntington Gardens.

"Maybe it was Maddox and his goons again,"

said Bea, watching their classmate sneak a second or possibly third donut. After all, the only crime they'd ever investigated before had been committed by Maddox and his three friends.

"Right!" exclaimed Teenie. "They started with petty theft and now they're on to parent-napping!"

Teenie swung the camera around to find the class bullies, Maddox, Memphis, Joe, and Jayden, pulling at their dress clothes.

"Is there anything you want to say to Simon and Miguel?" Bea asked.

"Our dads. This is their wedding."

"This is a wedding? Gross." Memphis seemed

truly surprised. "I've been to four of my mom's and dad's weddings. They're all boring."

"What kind of phone is that?" Jayden asked. "Does it do 4K video?"

Joe nodded to a llama piñata that was sitting under a tree. "When can I start hitting that piñata?"

"You have to wait for them to put it up," said Teenie from behind the camera.

"Oh, yeah?" said Joe, slugging his own hand with his fist. "Why?"

"Say, were we supposed to bring a gift or is our presence a present?" Maddox asked, smirking.

Bea, Teenie, and Oliver didn't trust these jokers, but they had to move on. They still had seventy suspects left to interview.

The rest of their class was a complete bust.

Their friend Rose couldn't talk even for a second. She'd seen Miguel working feverishly to hang the string lights over the dance floor and was now holding his ladder.

"Thank you, Rose. At least someone's helping." Miguel climbed down to see his daughters and Oliver making the wedding video, but nowhere near ready for the wedding.

"Girls!" he shouted, dropping string lights to the ground. "Have you seen your dad? Not only did he leave me to set up this entire wedding, he missed our couple's portrait session! Why get married if you're not going to take pictures?"

"You could always take pictures without him," Teenie suggested.

"I tried. But I kept feeling like there was something missing.

"Anyway, you've got to get ready!" Miguel said to his daughters. "The wedding is in . . ."

Rose checked her digital-pet watch, which she used even though the tiny computer gave her an allergic rash.

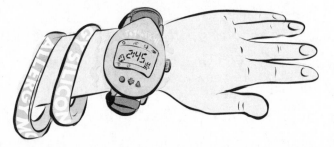

"Fifteen minutes, Mr. Miguel."

"What's the point of getting ready?" Bea asked

as they headed back to the mansion. "We haven't found Dad."

"Maybe Dad is just getting ready somewhere else," Teenie said hopefully.

"But we've looked everywhere!"

"What about the kitchen?" Benny whispered in Oliver's ear. "The chef in there, I hear she chops up animals for stew."

Oliver looked at the line of caterers exiting the kitchen with trays of hard-to-identify meats.

He shuddered as a caterer offered him chopped liver. The girls grabbed chicken fingers.

"You're looking all over, but what if *he's* all over?" Benny speculated morbidly. "What if they're serving Simon everywhere?"

Oliver grabbed the appetizers out of his friends' hands.

"No time to eat! We've got to get ready."

Getting Ready (to Call It Off)

The video crew reconvened in the family suite, where their outfits were hanging on a rack. The twins' dresses matched the lining of Simon's suit, which was a nice detail but made little sense, as no one would see the lining except them.

Teenie really didn't want to wear a dress, but she'd agreed to it as long as the dress had a sash for her flower sword. A flower assassin needs a flower sword. It wasn't sharp, but it would knock the petals off a flower if she swung hard enough.

"WAIT!" Bea pointed to her father's suit hanging from the top of a tall closet door. "Dad's suit.

What if there's another clue inside it?"

The suit was too high up for any one of them to reach. But Teenie insisted it would be possible if the others climbed on her shoulders. Oliver thought this was a terrifying idea, but he agreed to take the highest position because he was the smallest and lightest.

Lifted to more than twice his height, Oliver could see dust on the shelves and cobwebs on the ceiling, but no kidnapping-related clues. He grabbed Simon's jacket and handed the pants down to the girls.

138

"Check to see if he's got any cash in there," Benny suggested.

"I'm not stealing!"

"Of course not," said the wise rabbit. "It's just . . . ransom money."

Oliver swung the jacket around, checking the interior pockets and sleeves for ransom money. He had his arms all the way through the jacket when he heard Miguel exclaim:

"Oh, there you are!"

Teenie jumped in surprise. Oliver was certain they were about to fall, but she steadied herself, and they all hid behind Simon's suit.

"Well, Simon?" Miguel continued. "Where have you been and where did you get that ridiculous top hat? Bad enough the girls are making us wear Halloween ties."

"Oh no," Oliver whispered to Benny. "He thinks we're Simon! If he finds out Simon is really gone, they'll call off the wedding."

"I've got an idea," Benny whispered back.

The rabbit cleared his throat. "We're not supposed to see each other before the wedding!" he declared loudly. "It's bad luck."

He sounded exactly like Simon! Oliver was astonished, until he remembered that Benny had done impressions on the Vegas stage.

"I thought we weren't bothering with that, but if you insist . . ." Miguel turned around, so he was no longer facing Simon's suit. "What are you doing up here, Simon?"

"I'm just, um, writing my vows."

"Ugh! We vowed no vows!" Miguel threw his hands up. "Now that's one more thing I've got to do! The wedding's in ten minutes, Simon. And we still need to take pictures. You really know how to create a scene, don't you?"

Miguel stormed off, stomping loudly down the stairs.

Once the coast was clear, the twins helped Oliver to the ground. Well, Bea wobbled, and everyone fell.

"I didn't know you could do impressions!" Bea exclaimed.

"Yeah, that was way better than your magic," Teenie said. "No offense."

Oliver looked at Benny, who'd crushed his tail during the fall. The rabbit cursed and hopped with his hat toward the exit.

"For a second, I thought it was your rabbit talking," said Bea.

"HA!" said Oliver, a little too loud. "Benny talking. That's funny."

He picked up the rabbit and pretended to pet him as he closed his hand over the rabbit's mouth. Oliver felt the nip of two very large, sharp incisors. "Ow!"

Free again, Benny jumped from Oliver's hands onto a shelf that held two flower bouquets and two baskets of petals. The flowers looked delicious.

"Benny!" Bea shouted. "Don't eat their flowers!"

Oliver tried to grab Benny, but just as his hand reached the rabbit's fur, Benny, the flowers, and the entire shelf disappeared. An ancient pulley system was revealed in the open wall.

"Another trapdoor!" Teenie exclaimed.

"That's a dumbwaiter," Bea explained.

"Don't say *dumb*. It's rude."

"No, that's its name. Old houses have them. It probably goes to the kitchen. I bet that's where Benny winds up."

"Oh, good," said Teenie. "He'll be safe, then."

Oliver ran from the room before the twins could say another word.

"Don't forget the flowers!" they shouted after him.

As Teenie swung the sash and sword around her waist, something was knocked out of her pocket. It was the envelope with their names scrawled across it.

"If we can't find Dad, there won't be a wedding," said Bea, picking up the envelope. "We might as well open this now."

Since there was only one envelope to open, the twins naturally had to open it together. "One . . . two . . . *three*!"

The envelope ripped apart along with a puff of smoke.

Inside was a single page with a collaged request.

"It's got the cool letters!" exclaimed Teenie. "Just like I wanted!"

IF You waNT To SeE youR FaTHer AgAiN, PLaCE TWo, No, THree HuNdred DoLLaRs baCk in the BIRDCAGE

"Yep, it's a real ransom note," said Bea, reading carefully. "How are we going to get three or even two hundred dollars? What are we—millionaires?"

15

Rabbit Down the Hole

Having spent so many years in show business, Benny had seen worse elevators than this dumbwaiter. Still, he was worried. As a rule, he avoided kitchens. And the Hauntington kitchen was, according to the rat, notorious.

Benny hid in the basket of petals. If someone saw him, he'd be camouflaged—as an Easter Bunny. He gagged at the thought. Easter Bunny?! Never get him started on the Easter Bunny.

It wasn't long before the dumbwaiter landed with a thud and Benny could see into the bustling kitchen.

In the center of the room stood the chef, a tough-looking woman in stiff chef's whites, holding a cleaver high above her head.

Uh-oh.

The cleaver slammed down on the counter.

Then Benny saw it: the largest bowl of salad he'd ever encountered. It had everything: carrots, cherry tomatoes, water chestnuts, broccoli, cauliflower, bok choy. He was in heaven. Or fifteen feet away. He just had to get across the kitchen without being noticed.

"AAAAHHH!" a caterer screamed. "There's a rat in the dumbwaiter."

Benny thought about correcting him. In his line of work, the worst thing you could be called was a rat. However, explaining would likely make it worse.

He hopped over to the salad. If he was going down as a rat, he'd eat like a rat first.

The catering staff was so scared of this giant, elevator-riding rat that they all ran away. But not the chef. And she was fully capable of making rabbit stew all by herself.

The chef pointed her cleaver at Benny. "Don't even try it."

Just as the chef was about to pounce on the rabbit, Oliver threw himself between them and pulled Benny away from the salad bowl.

And Benny didn't get a single bite of bok choy.

Worse yet, he had to suffer another hug.

"Everyone gets so emotional at weddings," Benny complained.

Oliver was just glad to have his bunny back.

The chef put down the cleaver and clapped her hands to get Oliver's attention.

"You! What are you doing in my kitchen? And why are you hugging that rat?"

"Aaack! A rat?" Oliver jumped back and scanned the room.

"Psst, she's talking about me, dummy," Benny whispered.

"Oh, you mean Benny," Oliver said, relieved. "My bunny."

"Well, he scared my crew half to death," the chef said. "Now I've got to go collect those big babies. Don't touch anything! Especially not the cake. I know how you kids love cake."

As the chef walked out, Oliver could see the massive cake, in all its frosted glory, sitting in the open fridge.

"I guess nobody will notice if I take one bite . . ."

Oliver walked as if in a trance, not stopping until his nose was almost touching the multitiered, multiflavored mountain of his dreams. He decided he would take a sliver—just the tiniest morsel— from the bottom, where no one would ever look.

Cupping his hand, he attempted to scoop a handful of cake. He hoped the layer would be chocolate.

But it wasn't chocolate—or any other flavor. Under the frosting, the cake was rock solid.

It was a fake cake.

Why bake a fake cake? Did someone make a mistake?

He stepped back and examined the cake with a critical eye.

"Benny, how many tiers was this cake supposed to have?"

"I don't know," grumbled the rabbit. "But if you don't hurry up, I'm going to start shedding tears of boredom."

Oliver wiped away a circle of frosting where he'd tried to get his piece. Underneath was a shiny black surface. He knocked on it. It sounded hollow. He knocked again. This time something very strange happened.

The cake knocked back.

Oliver's eyes lit up. "Benny, I figured it out!"

He had cracked the case. Now all he had to do was crack the cake.

Cutting the Cake

The chef didn't believe that there was a man inside.

"A lot of people try to get me to give them a taste," she said, grinning. "But it's the first time I've heard that one."

"Please don't take the cake away," Oliver begged. "I swear there's a man trapped inside it."

"Sorry, we have to get it out to the floor. The baker said to let the cake chill for two hours, then take it out for viewing. That goes for anybody inside the cake too."

"*Please* don't take the cake away!" Oliver shouted as they took the cake away. "It's one of the grooms!"

"Oliver, calm down," Benny said. "Have a cookie to tide you over. You'll get cake later."

"I can't calm down," Oliver said. "Simon is inside the cake! I heard him!"

"Oh, why didn't you say so? That explains everything!" said the rabbit, who had seen plenty of

Vegas performers jump out of cakes. "Seems a little funny for a wedding, but to each his own. So when is he jumping out? When's the big reveal?"

"A reveal! Great idea, Benny! We'll make it another magic show."

Oliver found Bea and Teenie on the stage steps, comforting Miguel.

Behind them, rows of seats had been set up in two sections with an aisle down the middle. Guests stood around, talking awkwardly, pretending not to notice that one of the grooms was crying.

"Your father—you can't rely on him for anything!" Miguel said, sobbing. "I just saw him a moment ago in his suit, and now his suit is back on its hanger and he's gone! Is he really leaving me alone at the altar?"

"Don't worry, we have good news, Papa! Daddy didn't leave you . . . Or not on purpose," Bea qualified.

"He never does anything on purpose," their papa blubbered.

"He was kid—dad-napped," said Teenie.

"That's your good news?" asked Miguel, mid-sniffle.

"Well," said Bea, "it is if you pay the ransom."

"Ransom?! Did he put you up to this?"

Bea shook her head. "What if we told you that Dad could reappear for two or possibly three hundred dollars?"

They were about to show Miguel the ransom note when Oliver arrived with a counteroffer.

"I can make Mr. Simon reappear for free," said

Oliver breathlessly, wand in the air. "With magic!"

Bea and Teenie left their father's side to confer with Oliver.

"Oliver, Papa is really upset about Dad," Bea said, not quite out of her father's earshot. "I don't think magic is going to cheer him up."

"He has to pay all that money," said Teenie. "Or else get used to being a single parent."

"Not that being a single parent is bad," said Bea. "Your mom seems really good at it."

"And you seem pretty good with Benny," said Teenie.

"No, you don't understand," Oliver said. "We just have to cut the cake and everything will be okay!"

"Um, Oliver, we know you like cake, and we do too, but it doesn't solve everything," said Bea.

"Plus, even if it makes you feel better for a little while, you crash from all that sugar," said Teenie, clearly speaking from experience.

"No, just listen to me for a sec . . ." In a rushed whisper, Oliver explained what he'd discovered.

The twins' eyes grew wide. "And the baker seemed so nice! I guess you can never tell!"

Smiling, they gathered everyone around the cake, which now sat near the bar.

Oliver shushed his rabbit before stepping in front of the very large crowd.

"Ladies and gentlemen, friends and rabbits," said Oliver in his best magician voice. "As you see, this is a somewhat non-traditional wedding . . . because we're serving the dessert first. It's time to cut the cake!"

Getting a few reluctant laughs, Oliver shifted the mood and held up the saw.

"Brilliant Bea and Tremendous Teenie, will you divide the cake in half? Or however you think is fair."

The twins gripped the handles of the saw. They moved it back and forth across the surface of the cake, until they found a spot they could agree on. Then they went to work.

Now that the cake was cut in half, all the layers were revealed.

"May I have a few volunteers to taste the flavors?" Oliver asked.

158

He volunteered to go first.

"Hmm, that's funny," said Oliver as the others finished tasting. "Something is wrong with the last layer."

He wiped away some frosting, and tapped his wand on the solid bottom section of the cake. "Mom, can you help?"

"I told you, Oliver, I'm on vacation."

"But this will be a piece of cake!" Audience members laughed nervously. What was this boy doing? "Do you have your stethoscope?"

Diane looked confused, but she took out her stethoscope from her bag. Even on vacation, she was prepared for medical emergencies.

"I guess you can't hurt yourself too much with this," she said, handing it to her son.

Oliver placed the stethoscope's bell on the hard wooden surface of the coffin. It was just as he'd suspected.

"Phew," he said to himself. There was a lot riding on this last trick—including a marriage and a family and his reputation as a magician.

He handed the stethoscope back to his mother, who listened as well.

"This cake . . . This cake has a heartbeat!" his mother cried in astonishment.

Shifting into nurse mode, she pushed half the cake away. "We have to get this patient to surgery stat!"

Teenie was lucky to catch an armful of cake, along with a faceful of icing.

Resisting the urge to take some of the cake for himself, Oliver finally opened the lid of the coffin.

Simon sat up, blinking under the multicolored wedding lights. He looked dazed, but relatively un-harmed. Aside from the worm-patterned necktie tied around his mouth.

It was a big reveal indeed. The audience burst into applause.

Simon's daughters stared at him in amazement.

"Dad—there you are!" Teenie hugged her father.

"We thought you hated the magic show!" said Bea. "Who knew you were the grand finale!"

Oliver's mother shook her head. "I must say you're a good sport letting my son bury you inside a cake like that," she said to Simon. "I would never put up with it myself."

Still gagged, Simon made a muffled sound of protest.

"Sorry, I can't understand you with that silly tie in your mouth," said Diane, leaving the stage. "Who wears a worm tie? And on their wedding!"

Miguel ran over. "Oh, so now you decide to come out of hiding? No, don't say anything! You can apologize later. If we get married right this second, there will still be enough light outside to take pictures before dinner!"

As Miguel wheeled his husband-to-be toward the aisle, everyone stood and clapped even louder. What a way to begin a wedding!

Even Maddox seemed impressed. "That's the only way I'm ever getting married!"

"A standing ovation!" Benny marveled. "Kid, this cake trick is a keeper!"

Oliver grinned and grabbed a celebratory handful of cake.

The processional music began right on time: "This Must Be the Place" by the Talking Heads.

Bea and Teenie looked at each other in a panic. "Flowers!"

They'd been so involved with their detective work, they'd forgotten their most important jobs, flower scientist and flower assassin.

"Where are we going to find flowers now?" asked Bea.

Benny held up his paw.

Oliver suddenly remembered his job as well. "What about the rings?!"

Oliver grinned. "I knew those would come in handy."

"Oh, no, Papa is pulling the gag off Daddy's mouth," moaned Teenie when they joined their fathers under the canopy.

"What's wrong with that?" asked Bea.

"It means they're going to kiss!"

"Oh, no—let's not look!"

The Reception

The ceremony could not have gone better, at least in this family it could not have gone better. Oliver accidentally locked the magic rings together, but at the twins' suggestion, their fathers exchanged neckties instead, which everyone agreed was much more romantic. Sadly, in the chaos, no flowers were assassinated or scientifically studied; they were merely enjoyed.

Then, at last, came the family photos. Using a timer and a tripod to square his shots, Miguel hurried back into frame for each picture. It made for some funny faces, but the late-afternoon light was fantastic.

"Don't worry, there's no need to apologize for missing the original portrait time," Miguel said to his new husband. "We can talk about it later."

"Why should I apologize?" asked Simon. "There was no way I could make it."

"It's crazy the lengths people go to avoid having their picture taken," Miguel muttered.

"For now just say 'SORRY' for the camera," he shouted through his teeth. "Say 'SORRY,' everybody!"

From photos, they went straight into dinner. Half the crowd had spoiled their appetites on cake, so dinner went fast.

Speeches came next.

After their grandparents, it was the twins' turn.

"And now the reason we're all here today," Simon said. "They were the first to propose this marriage. Please welcome our daughters—"

"Dad, you don't know our new names." Bea handed her father a note.

"'The Brilliant Beatriz and the Tremendous Teenie,'" Simon read.

The crowd burst into applause. Once again, Bea and Teenie stole the show.

"Thank you, thank you!" they both said.

"This wedding really was a great idea, wasn't it?" the twins concluded. "Glad we thought of it. Cheers to the grooms, Daddy and Papa."

As glasses clinked in the air, dinner concluded. It was the traditional time for cake, or it would have been in a more traditional wedding.

Knowing this, Jacques Fondant arrived. For a work of art this size, he thought it best to cut the cake himself.

Instead, he found Simon's father, sidled up to the bar.

"Excuse me," he said. "I'm the baker, and I'm looking for the wedding planner."

"Sorry, I don't know from wedding planners," said Grandpa Bruce. "I'm the crime buster is what I am. And you're coming with me, buddy."

Having served forty years on the force, he had no problem guiding the large baker to the sweetheart table, where Simon and Miguel sat in front of their guests.

"There you are!" Miguel pointed his finger at the

baker. "Why'd you bake my husband into a cake?"

Jacques Fondant was confused. He'd baked a giant cake for both the grooms. He'd added a lot of buttercream and love, but he didn't bake anyone into it.

"I don't know what you're talking about," Jacques said. "I just came back to help you cut the cake."

He looked around. "But I see you already cut it. Did you release the dove?"

"What dove?" said Miguel. "We asked for a simple five-tiered cake, and instead you gave us ten tiers. One of which was my husband."

The baker was still confused. "But I only made

nine tiers. Lavender Vanilla. Original Orange. Raspberry Rampage. Blueberry Velvet. Cherry Lollipop. Burnt Caramel. Extra-Dark Chocolate. Raw Cookie Dough. Oh, and Coconut Countdown. Ten tiers—who could eat that much?

"See—" The baker pointed at the decimated cake. It was clear that the top nine tiers were just as described.

"But what is this tier at the bottom?" He swiped the bottom tier with his finger and tasted the frosting.

"Cool Whip!" he exclaimed in horror. "On a Jacques Fondant cake?! When I handed this cake to the wedding planner, there was no bottom tier. No husband. And most definitely no Cool Whip."

"But we didn't even have a wedding planner!" protested Miguel.

"Yes, we did it all on our own," Simon said. "Well, Miguel did. I was stuck in the bottom of your cake. Somebody hit me over the head and shoved me inside."

Oliver looked at the bottom tier of the cake, wondering who put Simon inside it.

The last tier was a wooden dolly, barely disguising the sawed-in-half coffin. It was only an illusion: a trick.

Suddenly, Oliver had a thought.

"Wait," Oliver said. "You said something about a dove. Was it the wedding planner's? Did he also have a mustache and a monocle?"

"Yes," said the baker. "And very full of himself he was too."

Suddenly, it all made sense. The identical boxes,

the ransom poem, the stolen groom, it was all the Great—

Wooden boards clattered and paper flowers flew as the wedding canopy collapsed under the weight of a single, well-fed dove.

Oliver pointed his wand at the frightened Zoocheeni. "Stop that magician!"

The wedding attendees looked from one magician to the other. They hadn't known there were two magicians at the wedding. One seemed more than enough.

With a poof of smoke, Zoocheeni and Paloma raced toward the exit.

But they weren't fast enough to avoid Simon's father, who tripped Zoocheeni with his cane and applied handcuffs to both the bird and the magician in one well-practiced motion.

"There's no such thing as a retired cop." Simon's father sighed. "Kids, if you'll excuse me, I've got to take this fella downtown."

"Sorry you've got to go, Pop!"

"Yeah, Dad, don't go!"

Simon and his sister Margie both made less than convincing attempts to stop their father from leaving.

Spencer had already brought the car to the valet

BEEDOOBEEDOOBEEDOO...

station, siren blaring. He wasn't about to pass up another chance to drive the police cruiser.

Grinning, he opened the door for Grandpa Bruce and the unhappy prisoners.

"Of course, it was Zoocheeni," said Bea as the police car disappeared through the Hauntington gates. "We should have thought of him immediately. He must have left the ransom poem and the ransom greeting card. But then who left the ransom text on your phone?"

"What ransom text?" asked Simon.

"The one that said you were in cold storage."

"I think it was the baker," volunteered Oliver. "He was talking about the cake."

"I wasn't asking you! But I admit that *might* make sense."

"What about Mexico?" said Teenie. "We thought you were going without us. We were so mad!"

"Oh! I almost forgot about Mexico," said their dad. "Where's the piñata I ordered?"

His daughters looked at him skeptically. A piñata was not the same thing as going to Mexico.

The piñata was still lying under the tree.

"Wait, does anyone have a stick to hit it with?" Simon asked, pulling the rope to lift the paper llama off the ground.

Miguel grabbed one of the posts that had held up the wedding canopy and handed it to his new husband.

The twins took the first turns attacking the spinning piñata, neither bothering to wear a blindfold.

"It better have the good candy," Teenie said.

"Yeah, don't try to get Smarties with us," said Bea.

"What's wrong with Smarties?" asked Oliver, taking the stick from them, and missing the piñata completely.

"Let's just hope there aren't any more fathers hidden inside," said Miguel.

One after another, their classmates took turns whacking the piñata.

Then Miguel, who still had a lot of pent-up energy but no more patience, grabbed the stick. With a final swing from Miguel, the piñata split open.

The kids rushed forward.

For nothing. There wasn't any candy at all.

Instead, a lone envelope dropped to the ground.

"Where's the candy, Dad?" Bea asked accusingly.

"Just open it," Simon said.

Teenie leaned in as Bea opened the envelope.

Inside were tickets for an all-inclusive family vacation to Mexico. The brochure promised rest, relaxation, and fun for the kids.

"I may not have planned the best wedding," Simon said. "But we'll have the best family-moon ever."

Miguel hugged his husband. Guests clinked their glasses and cheered.

As the crowd quieted, the music that Spencer had left playing seemed to grow louder.

"Well, that was exciting," said Miguel, breaking away from Simon. "Care to dance?"

Miguel and Simon had taken classes for a few weeks leading up to the wedding. In all the confusion, they'd almost forgotten the steps, but neither gave a single glance at their feet.

Benny tried to hide his eyes.
First with his sunglasses.

Then with his paws.

Finally, he could hide
it no longer. Benny
was crying like a baby
bunny.

"It's just all so beautiful,"
said the rabbit. "I love a wedding."

This was a surprise to Oliver, who'd heard Benny
complain endlessly about weddings.

However, it was a bigger surprise to Bea and
Teenie.

"You can talk!" Bea shouted.

"Of course he can!" Teenie said. "It makes so much sense that Oliver has a rabbit talking in his ear."

"It explains everything," agreed Bea. "There was no way he could learn all that magic on his own."

"Nobody can know," Oliver told them, his voice tense.

"Sure, okay," said Teenie. "We need to preserve your mystique. Nobody's going to hire you if they know you're not really a brilliant magician."

"Although it's a little selfish, taking all the credit," said Bea.

"No, you don't understand," said Oliver. "It's because he's on the lam. That's why nobody can know Benny can talk."

Benny wiped away his tears and got serious. "It's true. Every bookie in Reno is after me. All based on a misunderstanding, naturally. But they're wolves, all of them. So you gotta zip it, or they'll have me for breakfast."

The girls zipped their mouths shut as requested, but their silence didn't last long. They were being called to join their fathers on the dance floor.

"Mmon-ah-ay!" Teenie said with her lips still zipped shut.

"Huh?" came the response.

Bea unzipped her lips and shouted, "On our way!"

Benny was reduced to tears once more.

"All I wanted was one last dance," the rabbit cried. "But no, she left me at the altar and didn't turn back. We never danced again. *I* never danced again."

"And there you have it—two father-daughter

dances, side by side!" Spencer, who'd returned from the police station, was speaking into a scratchy microphone. "I think that has even broken the heart of a seventeen-year-old valet disc jockey. Now I need everyone to dance. That means grandmas. Grandpas. Kids. Rabbits. Everybody. You ready?"

Oliver couldn't refuse. His mother was already on the dance floor. Uncle Jeff too. The whole No-wonder third-grade class. Lita. Lito. Jacques Fondant. Aunt Margie. Simon. Miguel. Bea and Teenie. Everybody.

"The bunny hop!" Benny said. "How offensive. And they're doing it wrong. They don't even know the steps."

Oliver didn't know the steps, but he knew he wanted to dance.

"Benny, maybe you can join in just this once," Oliver said. "Show them how it's done."

He looked over to his friend, but Benny was gone.

He was already doing the bunny hop, and teaching everyone on the floor.

Oliver tripped over his feet a few times, but soon he too was dancing the night away.

The day may have begun with a man being sawed in half, but it ended with a family being brought together.

Weddings don't need magic, Oliver thought. They *are* magic.

BENNY'S BUNNY HOP

1 Stand tall. Hold the hips of the person (or rabbit) in front of you.

2 Stick your right foot out, and bring it back twice.

3 Stick your left foot out, and bring it back twice.

4 Take one hop forward, and one hop back.

5 Hop forward three times.

6 Repeat.

AFTER-PARTY:

SAW FOR YOURSELF

After this wonderful magic show and wedding, you may be dreaming of one day finding a special someone to saw in half. That day is today. You can saw for yourself.

You'll just need a few household items, a little practice, and a working knowledge of how to cut cardboard safely.

THE SAWED-IN-HALF TRICK: HOME VERSION

1. A shoe box

2. A pair of scissors

OK...

3. An adult's permission to use the scissors

4. Tape

5. Construction paper
(best if same color as shoe box)

6. Two very similar dolls or action figures with heads, feet, and other moveable parts still intact

7. A gullible audience

MAKING THE COFFIN

Using scissors and
care, cut the shoebox
down the middle. Cut
the lid as well.

Cut additional holes in the sides of the box. This
could be difficult and you may damage the box. Use
tape for any necessary repairs. It's fine to simply cut
out one flap on each side, big enough for the doll's,
or action figure's, feet or head to poke through.

Your box will now be open at the middle. Use construction paper to cover the open sides.

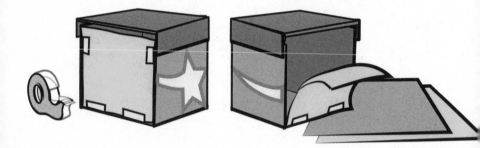

The setup is complete!

You transformed a lowly shoebox into a magical coffin. This is a good time to decorate. I recommend glitter. But it's your funeral.

PREPARE FOR THE TRICK

Hide one doll inside the foot-side of the coffin. (This doll will later provide the feet for the doll that is sawed in half.) Then put both sides of the coffin back together, and place the coffin on a table or stool.

Place the other doll in the audience, raising their hand in the air. This doll will be your volunteer and provide the head in the sawed-in-half trick. Now gather the rest of your audience, along with a few additional dolls or action figures, just to make sure it doesn't look like a setup.

SHOWTIME

You're ready to perform!

Start with some "patter," which is magician talk for, well . . . talk. Tell a joke or simply stick to the script: "I'm about to perform a dangerous feat of magic and daring, not for the faint of heart. Do I have a volunteer?"

Do not choose any living creatures who happen to volunteer. Choose the plant (I mean doll) you positioned in the audience earlier.

Engage the doll in some small talk.

Now ask your audience to cover their eyes as your volunteer prepares for the trick.

Place the volunteer doll inside the head-side of the coffin, positioned so that the doll's head sticks out, while the legs, and the rest of the doll, are hidden inside.

At the same time, maneuver the second doll at the foot of the coffin so that the doll's feet stick out of the other end. At this point, it should look like there is only one doll and only one coffin.

Your audience may open their eyes.

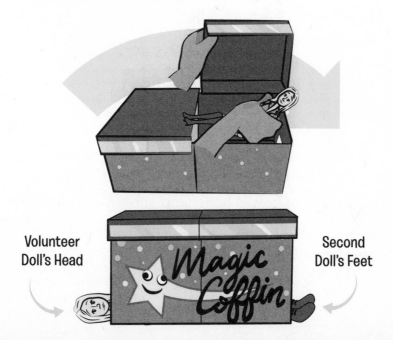

Volunteer Doll's Head

Second Doll's Feet

Magic Coffin

Reminding your audience that this trick is not for the faint of heart, take out your scissors. Cut another piece of construction paper to prove that they're sharp.

Say some comforting words to your volunteer doll in case the doll is nervous. Then cut the coffin right down the middle. You already did this, so it should be easy. Make it look difficult, though. Remember, the audience thinks you're actually cutting a doll in half.

Once you slice through the coffin, you should pull the two halves apart and show your audience what you've done. Ta da! This is a good time to check in with your volunteer.

Explain to the audience you're about to do something even more incredible: Put the volunteer back together again. You can talk about how you're doing this with "no medical training or anesthesia."

Push the two halves of the coffin back together with a magic word like "Voila!" or "Gesundheit!"

Now remove the doll from the first half of the coffin, unharmed. Take care to hide the other doll's feet at the same time.

Congratulations!

You've sawed your first volunteer!
Now hurry and put the scissors back where
you found them, but don't run!